Note: All activities in this book should be performed with adult supervision. Common sense and care are essential to the conduct of any and all activities, whether described in this book or not. Neither the author nor the publisher assumes any responsibility for any injuries or damages arising from any activities.

KINGFISHER
a Houghton Mifflin Company imprint
222 Berkeley Street
Boston, Massachusetts 02116
www.houghtonmifflinbooks.com

First published in 2006
2 4 6 8 10 9 7 5 3

Edited by Jane Casey
Designed by Katy Walker

LIBRARY OF CONGRESS CATALOGING–IN–PUBLICATION DATA
has been applied for.

ISBN-13: 978-0-7534-6041-2

Printed in China
2TR/0107/SNPEXL/MA(MA)/140MA/F

How to be a Pirate in 7 days or less

Illustrated by Jan Lewis
Written by Lesley Rees

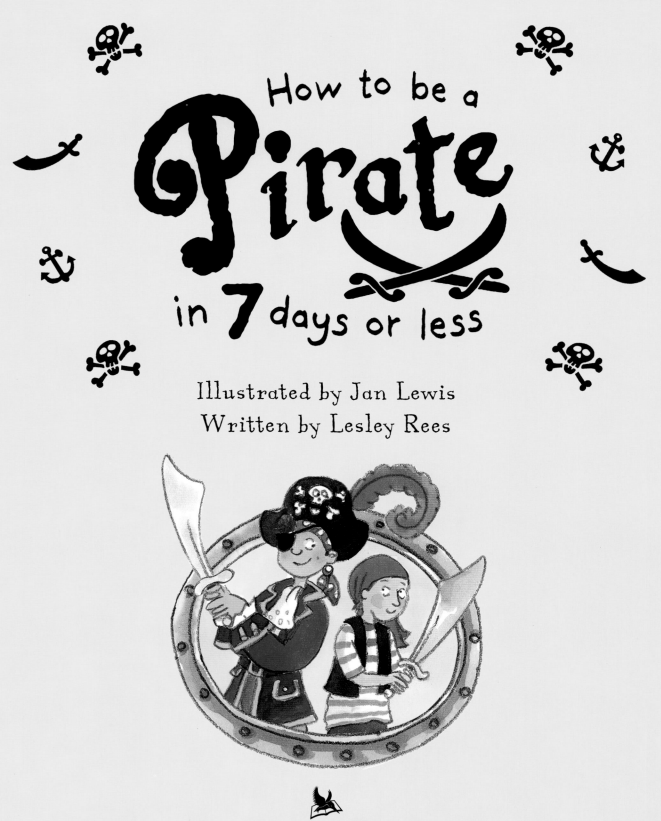

KINGFISHER
BOSTON

AHOY THERE!

Welcome aboard the *Jolly Roger*, shipmates. I'm Captain Kid, a fearless pirate, and I'm looking for a new crew! I'm here to show you how to sail the seven seas in search of trouble and treasures. In just seven days, if you follow my rules, you can become a pirate too.

Meet the crew!

Arrr!

Poopdeck is our noisy parrot.

I'm the captain of the ship, so everyone has to do what I say!

This is my first mate, Barnacle Billy. He's not afraid of anything.

We sail the seas looking for ships to raid and treasures to share.

Set sail with us, me hearties, and in one week
we'll turn you into a fearless pirate with your
very own cutlass. At the end of the week,
you and your crewmates can celebrate with
a pirate party. So shiver me timbers—
it's time to come aboard!

BRAVE BUCCANEERS

Every aspiring pirate needs to think up a pirate name before starting their life of plunder and peril. Pirates choose names that tell other people something about them— I'm Captain Kid because I'm the youngest pirate captain around.

See if you can figure out how these famous pirates got their names:

Blackbeard

Forkbeard

Little Jack

Bluetooth

Pegleg Pete

You'll need to choose a good name before you can call yourself a real pirate—try putting "Captain" in front of your first name.

PORTHOLE DOORPLATE

Make sure that everyone knows your bedroom is the captain's cabin with this porthole doorplate!

WHAT YOU NEED:

- a pencil
- 1 large bowl
- 1 smaller bowl
- 2 pieces of cardboard
- scissors
- glue
- a coin
- paintbrushes
- gray and black paints
- markers

1. Trace around the rim of the larger bowl on both pieces of cardboard.
2. Carefully cut out both circles. You may need an adult to help you do this.

3. Take the smaller bowl and place it inside one of the circles. Trace around the rim.
4. Now cut out the center of the circle in order to make a ring shape.
5. Spread glue over the back of the ring and stick it on top of the other circle.

6. Trace around the coin at even spaces along the frame. These circles will look like the rivets that hold the porthole together.
7. Paint the whole frame with gray paint. Make the inside a lighter shade of gray and leave it to dry.
8. In the middle, write your pirate name. You can trace the letters at the back of the book.

9. Paint on a skull and crossbones—you can use the template at the front of the book.

Now stick it on your "cabin" door!

SHIVER ME TIMBERS

Now, shipmates, if you're going to be a pirate, you have to look like one. Let's raid Mom and Dad's closets, and we'll soon have you looking like a salty sea dog! Arr!

Roll an old pair of pants up to the knees or cut them so that they look ragged. Be sure to ask permission first!

Put on a vest or jacket, with a belt tied diagonally over your shoulder in order to hold your cutlass in place. Now tie a scarf around your head.

Add a baggy shirt or striped T-shirt and tie a scarf around your waist.

Some pirates went barefoot, but others wore long, white socks. Wear them with black shoes, and you'll look pretty piratey!

Awk! Nice earring!

Don't forget the finishing touches! Your pirate hat, eye patch, and earring are in the pocket at the back of the book. Press out the earring and slide it onto your ear. Put on your eye patch and pirate hat. Now you're a swashbuckling scoundrel!

CUTTHROAT CUTLASS

A pirate's best weapon is his cutlass. It has a long, shiny blade, and it's razor-sharp. To be a real pirate, you need to have a cutlass. Why don't you make one that looks just like mine?

WHAT YOU NEED:
- thick cardboard
- a pencil
- scissors
- paintbrushes
- brown paint
- tinfoil

1. Copy the cutlass shape from inside the front of the book onto a piece of cardboard.
2. Carefully cut it out—you may need an adult to help you do this.
3. Paint the handle with brown paint.
4. Cover the blade with silver tinfoil.

And that's it!

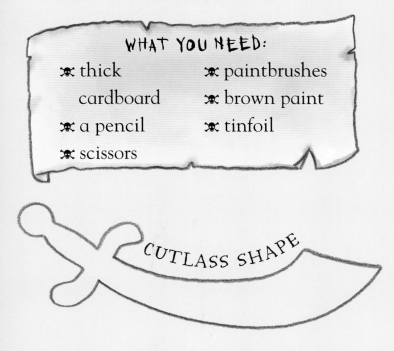

CUTLASS SHAPE

PERMISSION TO BOARD

Why do pirates sail the high seas looking for ships to raid?
To capture the jewels and money that they're carrying, shipmates!
Check out the tools that Billy and I use to help us find other ships.

I figure out where to steer the ship with my compass. Planet Earth is like a giant magnet—it makes the needle of my compass point north, so I always know the direction I'm sailing in.

Billy climbs up to the lookout and uses his telescope to spot other ships.

When Billy spots an enemy ship, we speed toward it as fast as we can. When we've caught up with it, we attack with stink bombs and cannons.

I spy a treasure!

We capture everything we can—gold, silver, jewels, or even the ship!

"I SPY" TELESCOPE

Now make your very own telescope.

WHAT YOU NEED:

- ✖ two cardboard tubes
- ✖ tinfoil
- ✖ scissors
- ✖ glue
- ✖ a ruler (inside the front cover)
- ✖ a paintbrush
- ✖ black paint

1. First, make sure that one tube fits inside the other one.
2. Paint both tubes black and leave them to dry.
3. Cut two strips of foil 2 in. (5cm) wide. Glue one strip around each end of the larger tube.
4. Push the smaller tube inside the larger one. You can slide it in and out, just like a real telescope. Easy!

LOVELY LOOT

We pirates take everything that we can use when we capture a ship—even the ropes and sails—but we can't carry all of it around with us. We need to find a safe, secret place to keep our loot!

There's not much room on a pirate ship, so we bury our treasures inside chests instead!

TREASURE CHEST

This is how to make your own treasure chest.

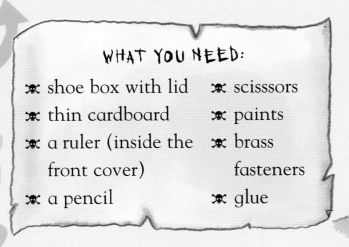

WHAT YOU NEED:

- ✖ shoe box with lid
- ✖ thin cardboard
- ✖ a ruler (inside the front cover)
- ✖ a pencil
- ✖ scisssors
- ✖ paints
- ✖ brass fasteners
- ✖ glue

1. Paint the box and lid with brown paint and leave them to dry.
2. Cut two strips of thin cardboard, 16 in. (40cm) long and 2 in. (5cm) wide.
3. Cut one end of each strip into a point.

4. Paint each strip gray and leave them to dry.
5. Put the lid on the box. Glue the strips to the back of the box and across the lid so that the pointed ends hang over the front.

6. Lift the lid and fold it back. This creases the cardboard strips and makes a hinge.
7. Push the brass fasteners through the box in rows, like rivets. Fold back the fasteners to hold them in place.

8. Paint your initials on each end of the box. You can trace the letters at the back of the book.

Now you have your very own treasure chest. Why don't you fill it with chocolate coins and jelly-bean "jewels"?

You have to hide your treasure chest in case someone else steals it.

Just be careful that you don't forget where you buried it! "X" marks the spot.

Sometimes pirates weigh down their treasure chests with stones and hide them at the bottom of the sea. Barnacle Billy and I buried our treasure chest on a desert island.

TREASURE MAP

When Barnacle Billy and I buried our treasure chest, I drew a map showing exactly where we'd hidden it, just in case we forget.

I drew the shape of the island and all of the important features—such as the palm trees. Then I drew the volcano that was close to where we buried the chest and marked the spot with an "X."

TIME TO PARTY

It's time to make the invitations for your pirate party. Why not make each one look like a treasure map, just like mine?

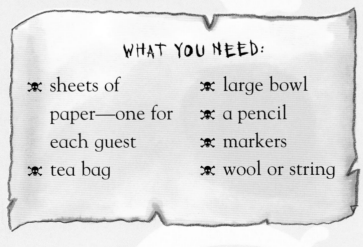

WHAT YOU NEED:

- ✖ sheets of paper—one for each guest
- ✖ tea bag
- ✖ large bowl
- ✖ a pencil
- ✖ markers
- ✖ wool or string

1. Put a tea bag in a large bowl and cover it with hot water. You may need an adult to help you do this. Leave it to cool.
2. In pencil, draw a map of where you live on one side of each piece of paper.
3. Draw a pirate ship where your house should be.

4. Draw a pathway with a dotted line that leads to your pirate ship/house and mark it with a large "X."
5. Scrunch the sheets into balls to crease them and dunk them in the water.
6. Unfold the balls carefully and lay them out flat to dry.
7. Tear the edges of the paper to make them look old.
8. On the blank side of each sheet, write out your invitation with markers. Write something like this:

AHOY THERE, SHIPMATE!
You are invited to a
Pirate Party!
on board
The Jolly Roger
(your address)
On
(date)
at
(time)
from
(your name)
Please dress like a pirate
(or walk the plank!)
R.S.V.P.

9. Roll up each invitation and tie a piece of wool or string around it so that it looks like an old scroll.

And that's how easy it is to make your invitations. The hardest part is deciding who to invite!

Don't forget to invite me!

THE JOLLY ROGER

Pirate flags are flown in order to terrify other seafarers. The pictures on them warn sailors that fierce pirates are on board! Let's take a look at some pirate flags.

The most popular flag is the Jolly Roger. It's red—the color of blood!

Pirates sometimes played sneaky tricks. They would fly a friendly flag until they were close enough to attack.

Flags feature different images. Some have cutlasses on them.

Some flags feature swords and hearts.

Some are decorated with scary skeletons.

FUN FLAGS

So how about making some flags of your own, shipmates? They'll look great at the party.

WHAT YOU NEED:

- ✖ sheets of paper
- ✖ a pencil
- ✖ red paint
- ✖ black paint
- ✖ glue
- ✖ a paintbrush
- ✖ straws

1. Draw your design onto a piece of paper. You can trace the skull and crossbones at the front of the book.

2. Paint the background black or red, leaving your skull and crossbones white. Lay it out flat to dry.

3. Spread a line of glue along one side of your flag. Place a straw next to the glue and fold the glued edge over it.

4. Press down firmly and leave it to dry. And that's it—your very own Jolly Roger! Why don't you make a few more in different colors?

GREAT GRUB

Being a pirate is hard work. We need plenty of yummy food to give us energy for climbing the rigging and leaping onto other ships. But pirate food can be disgusting!

We sail around for months without stopping, so most of our food is rotten. My plate is always full of maggots!

Our biscuits, called "hardtack," are full of wiggling weevils.

We love fruits and vegetables, but we hardly ever get to eat them.

If pirates don't eat fresh fruits, they can get scurvy, a horrible disease.

Let's make some pirate grub for your pirate party!

SCURVY-BUSTING GROG

WHAT YOU NEED:
- ☠ lemon-flavored soda
- ☠ orange juice
- ☠ ice cubes
- ☠ slices of oranges and lemons

1. Empty a bottle of lemon-flavored soda into a pitcher.

2. Add a small carton of orange juice.
3. Stir to mix.
4. Add ice cubes and slices of oranges and lemons.

Result—no scurvy!

HARDTACK

WHAT YOU NEED:

- ☠ sugar cookies
- ☠ powdered sugar
- ☠ jelly beans
- ☠ cold water

1. Place some powdered sugar in a bowl and add enough cold water to make a smooth paste.
2. Spread some of the mixture onto one side of a sugar cookie.
3. Place the jelly beans on top of the frosting—they're the weevils!
4. Leave to set.
5. Gobble them up, especially the weevils!

TOPSAIL SANDWICHES

WHAT YOU NEED:

- ☠ sliced bread
- ☠ peanut butter
- ☠ jelly
- ☠ toothpicks
- ☠ slices of melon

1. Spread peanut butter or jelly on one side of a slice of bread.
2. Cut the bread into four triangle shapes.

3. Push a toothpick through each triangle.
4. Stick the toothpick into a melon "boat" to form a sail.
5. Eat the sail first and then the boat!

DOUBLOONS, RATS' TAILS, & PIECES OF EIGHT!

WHAT YOU NEED:

- ☠ gold and silver chocolate coins
- ☠ licorice

Put the coins and licorice on a plate and let your friends raid it!

CANNONBALLS

WHAT YOU NEED:

- ☠ marshmallows
- ☠ bar of chocolate

1. Melt the chocolate in a microwave. Ask an adult to help you do this.
2. Dip the marshmallows into the chocolate and leave them to set.
3. Pile up your cannonballs on a plate and enjoy!

LET'S PARTY, ME HEARTY!

You've had a busy week learning how to be a real pirate like Billy and me. You deserve a reward. So let's celebrate with a pirate party! Get all of your crew together—it's time for some pirate party games.

— PASS THE CANNONBALL —

WHAT YOU NEED:

✖ gold chocolate coins (for the prize)
✖ sheets of black tissue paper
✖ music

1. Wrap the prize in lots of layers of tissue paper. Try to make the wrapping look like a cannonball.
2. Sit your pirate crew in a circle.
3. Play some music and pass the cannonball around until the music stops.
4. When the music stops, the pirate who is holding the cannonball gets to take off a layer of paper.
5. When the last layer of paper is removed, the cannonball has exploded! The pirate who's holding it gets the prize.

— PIN THE FLAG ON THE SHIP —

WHAT YOU NEED:

✖ pieces of paper
✖ colored pencils
✖ a bandanna
✖ thumbtacks

1. Draw a ship on a large piece of paper.
2. Get each of your pirate guests to draw a flag on a piece of paper and write their initials on it.
3. Taking turns, tie the bandanna around each pirate's eyes and spin them around three times. They must try to pin their flag on the mast. The flag closest to the mast wins.

SPIN THE BOTTLE OF GROG!

WHAT YOU NEED:

☠ a bottle   ☠ a list of tasks

1. Sit your pirate crew in a circle.
2. Place an empty bottle in the middle of the circle.
3. Take turns to spin the bottle. When it stops, whoever is sitting across from the open end has to do a task (such as standing on one leg for a whole minute or reciting the alphabet backward). If they complete the task, they stay in; if they don't, they're out! The winner is the last pirate left in.

CAPTURE THE FLAG

WHAT YOU NEED:

☠ a large area, outside or inside   ☠ 2 pirate flags

1. Divide your crew into two teams.
2. Mark three areas—one for each team and a middle "neutral" space.
3. Each team gets five minutes to hide their flag somewhere in their area.
4. To win the game, you must capture the opposite team's flag and bring it back to your area. If you are caught in the opposition's area, you get taken to jail (a special place within their area).
5. You can be freed from jail if one of your team members taps you.

Got it! We win!

Remember, no punching, kicking, or hitting!

TERRIFIC TREASURE

Yo ho ho! Did you enjoy those games? Great!
Now it's time for the treasure hunt! First you'll need
to draw a big map, and then you can add a few clues.

Hide your treasure in your house or yard. Mark the place on the map with a big "X," and then work backward to the beginning of the hunt, adding picture clues. Describe everyday objects around your home in a piratey way. Mark the path with small crosses.

Get the idea, shipmates? Keep adding clues until you get to the place that you've buried your treasure. Make sure that you bury enough treasure for all of your crew to share, or else you'll have a mutiny on your hands!

Desert island

Enemy ship

Sea

Coral reef

Now for some more fun and games, me hearties!

PIRATE TUG-OF-WAR!

WHAT YOU NEED:

☠ a long rope ☠ a bandanna

1. Divide your crew into two teams.
2. Tie the bandanna in the middle of the rope.
3. Mark two lines on the ground.
4. Each team holds one end of the rope. The captain shouts, "Heave ho, me hearties!", and both teams pull hard on the rope.
5. The first team to pull the bandanna over their line wins.

DRESSING-UP RACE

WHAT YOU NEED:

☠ a selection of pirate clothes

1. Spread the pirate clothes on the ground. Make sure that there is a whole outfit for everyone.
2. Mark a finish line a few feet beyond the last items of clothing.
3. When the captain shouts, "Go!", the pirates run to the clothes in front of them and dress up.
4. The winner is the first fully dressed pirate to cross the finish line.

SAIL AWAY

So that's it! You are now a perfect pirate. Great job, shipmate! Barnacle Billy, Poopdeck, and I can leave you to it, knowing that you're ready to sail the high seas with your own crew.

But before we set sail, me hearties, we'll leave you with a few important rules to remember.

1. PIRATES ALWAYS STICK TOGETHER.
Don't fight with your fellow pirates. They're your best friends and the ones you can rely on the most.

2. EAT LOTS OF FRUITS AND VEGETABLES!
That way you won't get the dreaded scurvy! Eating fresh fruits and vegetables is the only way to be a healthy pirate.

3. BEWARE OF WEEVILS.
Always check your hardtack!
Those pesky weevils can get
anywhere.

One for you and
one for me!

4. BE FAIR!
Pirates are tough on everyone
else, but fair with each other.
Share your loot with the other
pirates on your ship, and they'll share
theirs with you—including their
chocolate coins!

And most importantly of all . . .

BE PROUD TO BE A PIRATE!

Arrr, shipmates, happy sailing!

ROUTE TO THE LOOT!

Play a pirate game!

WHAT YOU NEED:

- ☠ 2-6 players
- ☠ a die
- ☠ counters (from the pocket at the back of the book)

1. Each player chooses a counter and throws the die. Whoever gets the highest number goes first.
2. Move forward the same number of circles as your throw. If you throw a six, move forward six circles.
3. Follow the instructions on the circles—they can be good or bad! Climb up the masts and walk down the planks.
4. Take turns throwing the die and moving until one of the players reaches the treasure chest and wins!

Your food is full of weevils—walk the plank!

You've found a gold coin in your boot—throw again.

The wind is in your sails— climb up the mast!

START

Trace over these letters to add the finishing touches to your doorplate, treasure chest, and any other pirate projects!

Aa Bb Cc

Dd Ee Ff

Gg Hh Ii Jj Kk

Ll Mm Nn Oo

Pp Qq Rr Ss Tt

Uu Vv Ww Xx

Yy Zz

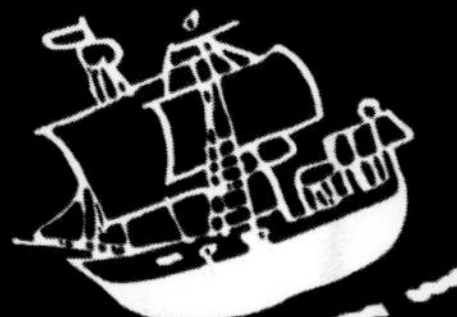